D1521999

Hi Shannon,

Enjoy my short story. You're the best! ☺

Virginia Ruella

May 2024

For My Sisters

Virginia Mueller

outskirts press

Outskirts Press, Inc.
http://www.outskirtspress.com

Hardback ISBN: 978-1-9772-3552-7

PRINTED IN THE UNITED STATES OF AMERICA

I dedicate my first novelette to my wonderful husband Tom, for his emotional support and providing me with some peace and quiet time, which has truly helped with completing this book. Thank you, Ava Coibion, my very first editor, and thank you to all of my friends, near and far.

ONE

It was three rowdy, loathsome juveniles and a mature individual that had taken advantage of the girls after offering to drive them home on a stormy rainy evening. They had other plans of their own. They drove the girls to a secluded location, a hidden place behind high boulders along a private ranch. The group of boys ignored the girls' plea to just take them straight home. The older male among them poked fun of them with jokes and raucous laughter. The more nervous the two sisters became, the more questions they asked about where they were being taken, the rowdier the group became. The drugs and alcohol they had been consuming all evening had driven them into a frenzy, and they found themselves raping and violently beating the sisters.

"Stop it! Stop it!" cries Sarah as Hector, a scheming, ruthless high school teenage dropout with a short barrel-chested body and scarred face, continues to beat down on her. After Hector's parents were sent to prison for being drug dealers, he lived off and on in foster homes. Hector was fifteen and had worked odd jobs throughout his life.

"Please stop," Sarah again pleads and cries from pain as she is lying on her side, doing her best to cover her bare breasts. She has little chance then of reasoning with him. As she lies with pain, her hair matted with blood, she turns to look towards her younger sister. Brittany lies in a fetal position on the ground, moaning softly, bleeding from her nostrils. Sarah can tell she is already semi-unconscious. Her thin body is bruised, dirty, and naked. Sarah, with her more heavily built body, has been able to sustain most of the beating. The eldest of her siblings, she has kept her athletic stature, always busy with the physical work of caring for her younger sister and brother. Her poor mother frazzled from holding two jobs after her father passed away from cancer five years ago. Her thoughts of her mom and glancing towards Brittany was unbearable. Sarah makes one more final plea to stop and leave them alone, softly crying. Slowly, it sinks in—she may not be leaving this place alive.

It was only when the girls went still, no longer fighting their captors, that Brian, the eldest, stood up and assessed the gruesome scene before him. "What have you done?" he shouted. "Look at them, they're dead!"

Brian grew up filled with bitterness and anger issues. He had lived his young life with his abusive father after his parents divorced. He maintained an athletic build due to many fights he endured in school.

"Just hold on one second! You're in this damn mess too, man," Hector yelled back. "Let's get the hell out of here before someone sees us." With this said, all four of them hurried off in Brian's car.

TWO

THIRTEEN YEARS LATER . . .

"Good morning, young lady. May I ask you where you think you're going with my nicest basket?" asked Gwen. "Oh Mom, it's a beautiful day. The park opens at nine. Robbie and I are heading there for a picnic," replied Betsy. "See, I packed sandwiches, chips, and these drinks. Okay, Mom? Please? We'll just be out only a few hours. I promise."

"Well, that sounds fine with me. Who will be driving you two?" asked Gwen. "Robbie is driving now. He's carrying his temporary driver's license, but in a week, he'll be getting the original," Betsy answered. "Oh Mom, he is super careful, and he has been driving the church's cart to carry senior citizens to the front door."

"I don't especially like that you're driving around with kids who don't have their driver's licenses. It makes me nervous. Okay I will approve it this time, only if you will return by one p.m., right after lunch-time, young lady. You must finish your packing. We head out by five this evening—your dad is getting us on the road early. He wants to avoid the rush hour heading back west, same as always." With this said, Gwen blew Betsy a kiss. Betsy heads to Robbie's car, which has just pulled into the driveway.

Robbie and Betsy had been relaxing already for three hours after arriving at Iowa's state-park—a peaceful, serene section for a quiet picnic while the radio played soft music.

A group of noisy men arrives. Betsy and Robbie survey them from a distance with an uneasy feeling. Within a minute, Eric and Duane had taken Betsy behind tall evergreen bushes while the others threatened Robbie if he tried to become a hero.

"You stupid jackasses," snarled Wayne. "All of you animals had just left the Bottom's Up bar not three hours ago, and here you are again! Luckily, my part-time job is to patrol this park area on weekends, and what do I see here! I am getting sick and tired of covering your asses. Eric, damn you, let her go! I mean it! Where the hell is Brian? That son-of-a—" "Here I am," said Brian, making his way from the other end of the pathway. Wayne points his finger at Brian. "Look, you shithead, just because I'm

your stepbrother and happen to be a law officer for the last ten years, this badge doesn't give me the right to just pretend this incident didn't happen, today or any other day. I told you before: you guys better clean up your act. I have threatened Robbie and he knows to keep her from crying about this. You all know what happened thirteen years ago, right? Enough of this damn shit already. I swear, I want to shut down that Bottom's Up 24-hours bar."
Wayne has a reputation of threatening to fabricate the ladies' reports of their assault against them. He threatens to charge them and make it seem that their only intention with the guys was to sell themselves as prostitutes, which would result in an embarrassing photo of themselves in the *Daily News*.

THREE

TWO YEARS LATER ...

Having graduated from college with a business management degree, Jacob accepted the day-shift supervisor position with GMC's auto mechanics department without hesitation. The job was in his hometown where he had grown up, so it made caring for his mother easy. Jacob was the youngest of three and unfortunately his two oldest sisters has passed away when he was only ten years old.

Almost as soon as he started, and to make some friends, he began engaging in friendly conversations with his fellow co-workers and the upper-management staff. Everyone was nice enough, but no one really showed any signs of wanting to hang outside of work to grab a beer, or to get a sandwich at lunch.

He had expected to make some friends by now. He needed a distraction. Without one, his mind always drifted to his sisters, and he became obsessive with the part.

Regardless, things were mostly going well; he was glad of having this position. As the charmer he was, Jacob had become friends with the Human Resources director, a lovely young lady who had given Jacob a list of the employees in the garage shop. He had become aware of the group of four odd guys that kept to themselves off in a corner when they were on a break, often laughing or talking in an animated way. Jacob strained to hear them, but sometimes it felt like they spoke in code. The group ate their lunch at the employees' picnic area outside, and it always seemed like they had some type of inside joke, rolling and howling like fools. The group always keep to themselves and seem very tight. Jacob noticed how they drove to work together, had lunch, and took breaks together. Heck, maybe they were even going to the restroom together. Jacob's most rewarding thought to himself after leaving the Human Resources Department: *BINGO*.

Jacob had not tried to get involved in their distant socializing, nor had he wanted to interrupt their breaktime. He prepared himself for rejection, which would not be a good thing. He decided to walk over to them to ask friendly questions. Surprisingly, they acted welcoming, answering everything he asked in an easygoing way and telling him at length about the best restaurants, clubs, and fishing holes that his new hometown had to offer.

Jacob makes it a point to routinely tell them what a great job they're doing, encouraging them to keep up the good work, and heads back to his desk to make the calls he has been putting off. Later that day, he asks his boss if he would be willing to consider a pay-raise for his team. Jacob thought that maybe this would be a way to make the group warm-up by making a raise possible for them. He has tried similar tactics.

For the past two weeks, he has been rewarding the shop employees with donuts and kolaches. Jacob could tell that the group felt good having him for their supervisor.

From time to time, Jacob chatted with the group of men, and gradually learned one particularly useful thing: they liked dating the ladies within the entire group.

A campground not often visited at this time toward the end of the summer season was Iowa's state park. He was expressing lots of interest in this new state in hopes of getting a tour of the place from the guys. He reminds the guys that he is a newcomer to this town and expressed interest in doing some fishing before the season was out. "If you have any suggestions as to good spots," he tells them, "I would appreciate it."

It was Monday of the week leading towards the final weekend of summer. The group, while on break, seems to appear excited. Jacob went over to see how they were doing, and they invited him to join them on a camping and fishing trip.

Perfect, Jacob thought. He places his hand into his pants pocket and presses his cell phone to ring. As the group looks on, he answers, talks for a minute, and hangs up. In the noisy shop, he replied in return that his mom called to remind him that he had promised that he would install four tires on her SUV and repair her timing belt. For the upcoming few days, Jacob would apologize repeatedly, reminding the group of how sorry he was for not hanging with them and for missing out on what he was sure would be a great time. He promised to join them next time.

And there was something satisfying to Jacob about knowing their fate but letting them live their pointless lives a little bit longer, in total ignorance of what was to come.

Jacob bought two tires in one day on the same week leading to the camping trip, while on his lunch-break hour. He made sure to save the receipt from the discount tire shop that was located near the GMC building.

From time to time, someone from the group would ask Jacob again, "You sure, boss, that you can't make it?" Jacob would always reply with a no.

The Friday before the weekend, Fred, Jacob's boss, and the shop's manager had just happened to walk by while the group was passing through. The group overheard Fred asking Jacob if he could help with the tire installation this weekend. "Thank you, sir," replied Jacob, "but my cousin offered to help me out this weekend. I really appreciate your offer." Jacob pretended to appear disappointed on account of having to miss the trip. He avoided a lengthy conversation with his boss. He was ready to go home, order pizza, and settle down with his *True Detective* DVDs he had ordered months earlier. As comforting as the thought was, he knew he was avoiding the world by living the way he did. He never seemed to go out and didn't date much. Maybe it had something to do with losing his sisters all those years ago and watching his mom struggle through life after their loss. Neither he nor his mother were over it. And maybe they never would be. Hopefully, someday his mom will get peace.

FOUR

The group was excited when it was time to clock out on Friday, and Jacob had watched them all day. He had convinced his boss and others who were listening that he had to service his mom's vehicle. The guys were just about to drive off from the employees' parking lot when Jacob caught up with them. He jogged up to Brian's truck.

"Hey," he tells them, "turns out I can join you for the weekend after all." He tells the guys that his mom very much would like if he goes and enjoys himself with his new friends. Since her club meeting had been canceled, she could wait until Sunday for him to do the repairs. "I'll meet you guys at the campsite in the morning. I will use the GPS for directions." With that, he hurried away out of the parking area.

Jacob planned on taking his Yamaha bike out for the trip. It was a gift after graduating from high school; his mom had not been able to afford a car. The bike had served as a dependable bike, supplying him with transportation to and from college. The bike also was dependable enough to have traveled the distance he made quite often out of town to visit his mom. A friend of Jacob's allowed him to keep it in his garage, so it had traveled well. The extra tank of fuel securely tied on his back railing always came in handy, and he would definitely fill it up before heading out on the camping trip. The more he thought about the trip, the more content and carefree he felt. Soon it would all be over. Maybe he could begin to live his life.

Jacob headed out incredibly early Saturday morning. He wasn't sure if the park was going to be packed with college students or families loaded with kids. He did read the newspaper before he left and found that at this time of the year very rarely did people extend their stay longer, as the season ended.

He arrived earlier than the rest of the group, and he managed to park his bike out of sight. He never liked taking chances with it and cared for it as much as he did the day he had received it.

As he waited for the group's arrival, thoughts ran through his mind. *Snowbirds*—the word that his dad once used to describe the incoming travelers during this time of year, just before passing away from cancer twenty years ago. The vacation-like environment of the campground made him think of the moment.

Or maybe because it was one of the last things his dad talked about, it stuck in his head. His dad had been telling him and his sisters that the tourists almost always head back home right before the fall season begins.

FIVE

An hour had passed after Jacob's arrival at 9 a.m. and still no sign of the group. Jacob continued with his thoughts. The temperatures were starting to drop. He considered the time change; darkness would be approaching fast this time of year. What a great relief it would be to feel the cooler weather when summer ends. The shade from under the oak, birch, and pine trees surrounding him had started to feel wonderful. He thought about the animals that all these tree-filled acres supplied refuge to and thank goodness this Iowa state park's administrative offices locked the gates after each summer. It supplied a safe haven for the wildlife from poachers. He remembered one childhood memory of his, of once finding two baby raccoons next to their dead mother and bringing them home to care for them. His sisters were so excited to have raised them and set them free.

Before Jacob's mom had moved to the West Coast, he remembered this beautiful two-hundred-acre park that is now Iowa's national state park. His mom was quite an outdoor person. She had known that this park's creek was fully stocked with bass, catfish, and bluegill. The creek flowed against a property line next to a reservoir that two other properties shared. Those structures were barely visible from the road, making the travel a wild and picturesque drive. He envisioned the picnic table his family once used under the red maples and aspen trees.

He didn't mind waiting for the group. It gave him more time to go over the memories he had of his sisters. It was something he made himself do all the time. He never wanted to forget a single moment with them, and he had vowed to himself that he never would. This he promised to do right.

SIX

The group traveled the three-hour drive Saturday morning as they had done many times before. Duane, a tall lanky hard drinker with a reputation as a danger-loving guy, packed ten pint-size bottles of gin and tequila for the road. His recklessness led him to the improper use of a semi-automatic that had discharged into his leg six years ago. The Army, to his great fortune, had discharged him on account of that injury while on duty. He had no further interest in pursuing a technical career, and moved in with his parents, where he had been collecting disability checks ever since.

The group, having consumed all the liquor during the commute, felt tipsy on their arrival by 11 a.m. The campground was the group's favorite place and most-often-used chill spot. Duane was thrilled that Brian and their group were able to take advantage of one more camping and fishing trip on the last weekend of summer. It beat being at home with his parents.

"Hey," Brian called out, as Duane was working his way out of the backseat of the truck. "Jacob's here already! And wow ... he even brought along breakfast. Come on, guys, get out of the truck. Let's get a bonfire going."

"Hey," said Eric to Jacob, swiping his long bangs out of his eyes. "We kept you waiting long?"

"Naw, wasn't a bad couple of hours," Jacob said, laughing and faking that he felt good while knowing the truth.

"Where did you park your car? Did you walk? Someone drop you off?" Eric fired off his round of questions.

"Can we skip the interrogation, Eric?" Duane said, rolling his eyes. Eric had never been his favorite out of the gang. He always reminded Duane of a weasel, and he was always obsessed with always getting his way. The way he brags about his disturbing ways of making out with his dates—disgusting. Some days Duane couldn't stand the demented look on his face. But he was part of the group.

SEVEN

Jacob just shrugged good-naturedly and replied, "Nope, I made it here over an hour ago, and just checking out the place. It's nice! And to answer your question, Eric, I rode my motorbike. I parked it out back, by the pine trees—I'm not taking any chances of having some hoodlum steal it."

Ha, Brian thought, *if he only knew*. Jacob seemed like a clean-cut kind of kid, so it probably wouldn't be good to fill him in on our way of having fun with the ladies.

Jacob steered them into neutral, passing everyone a beer. "So, how's everyone doing by the way? Some nice weather we have today. I brought some donuts and kolaches to satisfy our cravings before our next meal. What do you guys say we dig in, while they're fresh?"

The morning sun had risen over the trees as noon rolled in. Jacob passed a kolache to Brian and took the last one for himself. It felt good to provide the men with nourishment when he knew he was leading them to the slaughter. The way his uncle provided food to his litter of hogs before selling them to the butcher. While everyone was settling in around the campfire, Brian pulled out his iPad. "Hey man, why the iPad? I didn't even think you were able to get Wi-Fi out here," said Hector. "And aren't we supposed to be getting away from all that city stuff?"

"Sure, yeah. But I got data on this thing. By the way, did you bring more liquor?" Brian asked Eric. "Yeah sure," said Eric as he was looking into his backpack for more liquor. "I just can't wait to see the new porn site, man."

Brian went on, "This is the one I was telling you about. Go for it, Eric." "Don't forget me," Hector said. "I want to check out this new site, too. Besides, I heard it has the sweetest hottest babes."

But just as Eric began pulling up various sites, an advisory notice popped up on the screen. Jacob could just barely make out what was being said from where he was sitting.

Brian reaches for the iPad. "What the hell is this? Ah, man, I cannot believe this shit! A breaking news report just popped up. A breakout happened yesterday afternoon, one of their most high-risk prisoners escaped from the pen, the big place we passed up along the way the freaky eerie-looking one." "Ouch!" Hector laughed. "Bet those barb wires must have hurt."

Brian scrolled through the report and started to Google more news covering the story. "That place is only about forty to fifty miles from here. According to the reports, the dude was discovered missing on Friday's lunch hour. Well, why do I care, good for him. Bet he planned for someone to be waiting on the outside, man. It's always an inside job. Maybe a chick employee or some paid-off guard helped with the getaway."

"You're really getting into this stuff, aren't you, Brian," Eric chuckled. "But can we get back to the site?" "Sure, yeah. Getting it pulled up now. And let me tell you about the special lady I took out last night," as Brian winks.

Hector reached over and slapped Eric on the shoulder. "And I've got my date story from the other night that'll top his story."

Jacob laughed along with them, but the adren-aline-like feeling has started to come over him, dis-tracting him. He must continue to keep faking it, no matter what.

What a deranged set of people, thought Jacob, who had held on to his excuse of his mother's ve-hicle and let the group know he would come with them on another weekend. He had begun to feel nervous. He wasn't sure if he could do it. Maybe he needed more time. He sat on a log across from the group, not doing much of the talking, just taking in the river of thoughtless remarks.

And right before him, those jerks were obviously demonstrating and mimicking what they had done to their "so-called dates."

Increasingly intoxicated the four gathered closer together, and for a moment they forgot that Jacob was even there. They were cussing and bragging about their actions, comparing their dates in order to determine who had scored the best.

Wow, thought Jacob, *how disturbing are these guys! Each trying to outdo the other by being the best tormentor. Comparing notes as if they were actually learning valuable information. But they will be done with all that before long. They will never get to hurt another female again.*

EIGHT

Since he sat alone, in order to tune out the talk, he started to recollect back to his college days. He had been hard-pressed on becoming a psychiatrist in order to understand and deal with his past. Unfortunately, his memories haunted him more deeply than he had expected them to, surfacing more and more as he progressed through the coursework, and they began to disturb even his sleep.

For the past fifteen years he saved clippings of their past history, including saving the latest employment location of them all. After switching his degree from psychology to the business management route, he was able to fully concentrate on their whereabouts. These guys had been employed with GMC for five years now.

Being the new guy on this trip and not having related stories to contribute, he just listened. From time to time he turned his head away, a sick feeling forming in the pit of his stomach. Was it excitement?

Was it dread? Maybe it was a mix of both.

"Hey, Jacob. Hey man, you awake? Hey, wake up!" Hector shouted at Jacob. "You look like you were in a trance or sleeping with your eyes open."

Jacob replied, "Oh ... sorry, I didn't get enough sleep last night."

Hector continued, "So boss, now that we are not at work, you're one of us. Let's make this a fun week-end. How about you tell us what you like to do in your spare time. Do you have a girlfriend?"

"Ha. No. No girlfriend," Jacob replied.

"Maybe you work too hard. You're kind of young to be a boss-man. Right? Am I right? Guys, doesn't he look too young?" Hector looked at the others for comments but got nothing in return and focused his attention back to Jacob. "I have a personal question for you, man. Are you a virgin?" asked Hector, grin-ning. The rest of the group just stared at Jacob until Hector says, "I'm just asking a simple question, man. So ... I bet you're a virgin, huh? Yeah, I bet you are."

"Hey, jackass," Brian abruptly shot back to Hector, "be cool, all right?"

NINE

It was important that he fit in for now, and not wanting to come off like a wimp, Jacob replied, "You're wrong about that. I once dated two chicks at the same time." He couldn't suppress a blush at the absurd lie.

"Okay, now this dude is starting to relax," Hector said. "So, tell us about it—how did you get them to go out with you? Did you go at them from behind? Don't stop now, man—this is getting good."

Not wanting to take the questioning any farther in the event that he might slip up and give himself away, Jacob stood and cleared his throat. "Hey guys, have we thought about lunch?"

Despite Jacob's attempt to change the course of the conversation, Hector can't seem to resist, and prods Jacob again. "You know," he says, "if my girl doesn't wanna make out, I have my ways of getting her to. So, what is your method, man?"

"Hey, how about we get to thinking about our

lunch and worry about that some other time," Jacob answered.

"What the hell?" Hector snarled, rising to his feet. "I asked you a question, man."

"And I'm asking what are we having for lunch?," Jacob responded back.

At this moment Brian stood up. "He's right. How about me and Eric head to the creek to check if the fish are biting? If we hook 'em, we'll grill 'em for lunch. If not, we'll grill the sausage I brought. Why don't you guys make yourself useful. Get the grill out and have it ready. This is supposed to be a fun weekend let's show Jacob that chicks aren't the only thing on our mind," he laughs and winks to the group.

"Wait a minute, Brian. Wait just a minute. The fish for lunch is great. But tell me why you invited Jacob on our trip? I know he's our boss-man," said Hector, giving Brian a stern look, "but that's back in the shop, not here. You know the rules, it has always been just the four of us always! You broke our tradition and I don't like it, not one shitty bit!"

Jacob swallowed the lump in his throat and continued to stand in one spot, looking at everyone without saying a word.

Duane stood and moved closer to Hector, placing his hands on his hips, and shouted, "Let's not do this now and you wait a minute you dumb-shit and settle down, Hector. Besides being our new boss-man, Jacob is the new guy in town. He asked me if anything fun was happening this weekend. So, I invited him. What's the problem? Besides, if we play our cards right, and don't act like a dick, Hector, he might be able to give us an employee discount on those chrome rims we all want for our rides. Right? Am I right, Jacob?" he said, turning to Jacob, before returning his gaze to the rest of the group. "I'm not letting you mess up my chill time."

At this moment Brian turned to the group and said, "Duane is right." Then he tells Hector, "You talked me into coming out when I was just as happy staying at home, and that's about to be where I'll be heading if you don't knock it off. I'd rather still be at the shop, and all alone, than dealing with this crap." Then he glances at the rest of the group. "You're all a bunch of sissies, either kill each other right now or shut the hell up already." He laughs arrogantly, and Jacob wonders how much truth there is to this joke.

"Yeah, Brian, you're right," said Duane. "Besides, nothing wrong with including Jacob as a fifth guy in our pack if he wishes."

Jacob gave Brian and Duane a quick nod. He did not like where things were heading, not one damn bit. He would have to tread carefully.

TEN

Eric headed over to grab his fishing pole from the truck. "You know," he said, "it's going to be lunchtime in an hour or so, best we get a move-on."

"Okay then, let's get going!" Brian replied. As the two start their walk along the path toward the creek, Brian turns and tells the others, "Don't you guys go drinking up all the booze in the cooler, dog-gone-it. And keep an eye on the fire too!"

"So how far to the creek from here?" Jacob asked them both. Eric turned to face him, hefting a small pack onto his back. "Oh, it's about a twenty-five-minute walk. Why, you wanna join us?"

"Nope, I'll just chill here," Jacob replied, turning to converse with Hector and Duane as Brian and Eric finally were out-of-sight.

"What type of fish are in the creek, by the way?" Jacob eventually thought to ask but had known the answer. He continued to pretend he knew nothing of the place. Of course, he would be eating alone. A couple of fish on ice would fit nicely in his bike cooler.

"Have any of you eaten them before?" "What's with your questions, man?" laughed Duane. "You're tireless. Fish is fish."

"Well, since I've never been here before," Jacob replied, "maybe I may want to return and do a little fishing of my own. I hope the guys will have some luck and be back by dinner; you know, with the time changing and all, it will get dark before you know it. Just realized it's already a little late for lunch."

"Look, it's been twenty-five minutes already. Bet they cast in their hooks," said Hector. "Maybe if you got laid occasionally, you wouldn't be so uptight."

Duane laughed. "Yeah, you're as wound up as the last lady I took advantage of. There was nothing I could do to make that one relax."

Jacob couldn't take it anymore. He got up and headed away from them.

"Hey, where are you going, Jacob? Come on, man. Where are you going, dude? Come on back and tell us about the chicks you dated, man. Duane and I wanna hear all about it."

"Just give me a few minutes," said Jacob. As he headed towards the restroom, he listened as the two hothead, loudmouth losers rolled with laugher, impersonating how the ladies resisted their advances. Duane was pounding his fists into the ground while at the same time moving his pelvis in a humping motion, while Hector laughed and cheered him on.

Hector then began to talk about two teenage girls working at a new hamburger joint that opened a month ago. "Those chicks wear their tops so tight; their nipples are always hard and bulging out."

"Hey man, what do you think? Want to take them out?" asked Duane. "How about you and I show them how we party? Say next Saturday?"

Jacob watched from outside the restroom building as Hector nodded his head in approval. "Hell yes. It's a deal! Soon as we get back."

They both did a high-five motion. "All right! I can't wait either, but you do know that Brian will be joining us!" said Duane.

Jacob lingered just out of sight for another moment, and Hector and Duane suddenly changed the subject. Now both were bragging about an incident that had happened fifteen years ago. Jacob heard every word, taking in their version of the story. The details were sickening, but he needed to imagine what happened now that he had it all laid out in front of him.

He had hunted for clues for so long, so many years, and now the culprits had conveniently dropped right under his nose, by being his workmates. Jacob watched as Hector looked around secretively but couldn't see him in the dense bushes that hid him. Hector must have remembered that he and Duane were not alone and abruptly stopped, tilting his head and glancing over toward Jacob as Jacob was making his way towards them. Duane looked at Jacob, turned and whispers to Hector, "Hey, dude. Remember, we're not to talk about this shit. Especially not now you know Brian doesn't want any of this shit coming out. I mean, none of us do. But Brian would literally kill us."

Jacob in fact did hear their loud mouths. *He made it a point to eavesdrop.*

"Hey, Jacob," shouted Hector, snorting and spitting phlegm in the fire pit. "What the hell is taking you so long over there? Come on, sit right here." Hector patted the bench next to him. "Tell us a good story or something."

"Okay, okay," Jacob replied, composing himself. He had to play it cool. "Here I come. I had to take a leak, man. But I'm afraid you'll be disappointed; I don't have much in the way of stories."

ELEVEN

Meanwhile, Brian and Eric had arrived at the creek. "Hey man, what do you think of Jacob?" asked Brian. "I mean, do you think he will be okay to hang with us? He seems kind of cool. Besides, I think he does have a girlfriend, that hot chick he is always talking to at work. But hey, I think she'll leave him for me. Well, let me put it this way: I bet I can take her from him. Remember in July, the company picnic? I think she was checking me out."

"Well, I'm not sure about all that," said Eric, giving the creek a good look-over before casting his line. "What I really can't believe is that we're the only two guys fishing. I mean, this park is usually crowded with people on this last weekend of summer, packed with moms and dads and kids. You know, we should have brought our guns for some target practice," added Eric.

"Hell no," said Brian, shaking his head. "Just one loud shot from our guns and the park patrol will be all over our ass. But then again, if Wayne is patrolling this weekend, it probably would've been all right. Come to think of it, I haven't seen any patrol cars around. Which is fine with me, you know," Brian said.

TWELVE

Back at camp, Hector kept pushing Jacob until, finally, Jacob caved and made up a few lies to get the loudmouth off his back. He told them the first make-believe story that popped into his head. It was too late not to; he was here for the weekend and his agreeability made it possible for him to be accepted by these guys. Which now seemed more important than ever, if only for a little while longer.

He walked with his hands in his trouser pockets while standing in front of the fire but across from the two. He made himself appear as casual as possible before addressing an old incident.

"Oh, and by the way, Hector and Duane, why don't you two tell me about the incident that happened with the two sisters. The two girls you offered a ride because of the rain. You said it happened about fifteen years ago?"

"What is this shit?" grunts Hector. He and Duane both stood up and stared at each other for a moment with curiosity, their mouths agape. "How, I mean, what do you know about that? Who told you this crap?" Hector said nervously. Jacob could see he was wringing his hands into fists.

"Brian told me the whole story, like he was proud of it!" Jacob answered.

Duane was looking agitated as well, with his fists clenched tight. He stared at Jacob while trying to keep still and said, "Oh yeah? Doesn't sound like Brian."

"Sure sounded like him when he told me the story," quipped Jacob. "Looked like him too. Pretty shitty story." *I must sound convincing to these jackasses.*

"Well, just wait, because when Brian gets back, I am going to kick the shit out of his ass for telling lies!" shouts Duane. "He's been the one threatening us all these years."

"Forget about Brian and shut the hell up," Jacob said. "I want to hear your version of the events on how this went down. Just tell me why you four degenerates did this to the girls. And then answer me this: did any one of you feel any remorse, regret, what-so-ever?"

"Dude, those are some serious accusations," Duane said. His teeth were gritted, his fists tightly balled at his sides.

"Damn straight, this is some serious shit. Tell

me this: after raping them, was there really a need to beat them to death? Why didn't you just leave them alone? Why torture their poor bodies? You really thought you would get away with it? I bet that no-good stepbrother of Brian's you guys are always talking about had something to do with covering this up. Wayne helped you miserable jackasses get away with this, right? Am I right?" Jacob said angrily.

"Hey, look, man, Brian should not have told you nothing. This happened a hell of a long time ago," Hector said. "It's old news."

Finally, Jacob thought, *an admission*. He wanted to hear if they had any remorse, even if he knew it would not be genuine.

"Why do you even care anyway?" shouts Hector. "Tell us. Why do you care about this? Are you a reporter in disguise, looking for a story? You're only the new guy in town, not our boss today. We don't have to take this shit from you."

"Yeah, you better shut the hell up with this shit right now!" demanded Duane, pointing his shaky finger at Jacob.

At this moment, Duane and Hector both were making their move towards Jacob.

Jacob knew he would have to stay on his toes if he was to come out on top and give these filthy assholes what they deserved.

THIRTEEN

Meanwhile, back at the creek, Brian swung his cast, the line and hook landing ten feet from Eric's spot.

"Hey," Brian said, "I'm a little tired from all the walking and standing. I'm going to lean my rod against this rock and just sit myself right here, light up this joint, and watch you for a while. I want to enjoy this. This bag of weed wasn't cheap."

"Sounds good to me," Eric replied, adjusting his line and waiting for a bite.

Brian had just taken his first drag when they heard a loud *"bang."* Brian jumped up from his sitting spot and dropped the joint. Eric dropped his fishing rod into the fast-moving creek.

"What the shit was that? That was a gun fire going off, right? Do you think maybe someone came in for some target practice? What do you think, Brian?" Eric asked.

"Damn if I know," Brian said. "I just hope it isn't anything to worry about. I mean, maybe a couple of park patrols decided to come to the park after all. Maybe the patrol guys are messing around and shot a feral hog. I don't know, man. Hopefully, nothing weird is happening back at camp. Let's head back and see if the guys know what's up."

At this moment, a second "*bang*" had sounded off. Brian shrugged from the loud noise as a bunch of startled birds flew through the trees. "Maybe someone is out there doing some rabbit hunting or something! Come on, Eric, we got to get the hell out of here. I hate hunters, and I surely don't want to be mistaken for a damn deer!" Brian said.

Eric was too petrified to move. "Come on," Brian urged. "Which way is out? Damn, shit! I'm confused, man. And as many times as I been here? This can't be happening now."

Sounds could be heard coming from down the creek: the crackling of branches and rustling and crunching sounds of the nearby dry leaves and bushes. Not knowing what they were expecting to see appear from the forest, they both came to a halt.

"Shit, shit, shit," Brian mumbled, looking from side to side as far as he could into the forest and still feeling lost. "Someone or something is heading our way fast, Eric. Hurry!"

After walking several feet more, they heard the

sounds approaching faster and closer. Sharp loud rustling sounds, rapid groaning, and heavy breathing coming from right behind them. Both turned to look, and there stood Jacob stumbling forward, sweating and gasping for air.

"What the hell happened, man?" Eric demanded, firing off the questions spinning in his head. "We heard two, what sounded like gunshots go off. Did you hear it too? Where are the guys? Are they spooked?"

Jacob put his hands in his pockets and faced up toward the sky, catching his breath from running the half mile. Brian thought Jacob was assessing the chances of rain.

Jacob looked oddly more at ease than both Eric and Brian had ever looked.

"Yeah, I finally put those two filthy scumbags out of their misery."

There was a moment of silence before Brian said, "What the hell do you mean, man? What the hell are you saying? Tell me that those sounds didn't come from a gun you have to shoot our friends."

"That is so odd of you to say, and what makes you think I may have a gun?" Jacob said. "Did you say 'friends'? You are talking about those two dogs that are now dead back by the campsite, right?" asked Jacob.

"No way. What the hell, man. Tell us something real!" demanded Eric.

Jacob was feeling a little apprehensive because he wasn't sure if Brian or Eric was carrying a weapon. "You want me to tell you something real?" Jacob said, while reaching into his right-side trouser pocket.

But he had to be patient. He had to be smart about this. Luckily he had a second set of gloves on.

"No, you have it backwards," Jacob told them as he approached them. "I don't need to tell you a damn thing. But I do want you two to start talking about the torture, rape, and death of two young sisters fifteen years ago. I know for a fact you four beat the girls to death. You four are definitely guilty of the crime." His face turning red as he reaches for his Smith & Wesson. He pointed the gun in their direction. "So, tell me, right before you left them to die, were they crying for help?"

"Hey wait, man. Stop right there. No way did we kill them. We may have roughed them up, but they were alive when we left them," Brian muttered, glancing to Eric. "Yeah, dude," Eric said, nodding his head. "We left them alive!"

"Okay. So, you guys just roughed them up, like two human punching bags to beat on, then raped them," Jacob said.

"What's it to you?" Brian shouts. Jacob lifted the gun, alternatingly pointing it at Brian and Eric.

"Hey, wait a minute, man! Wait right there!" Brian cries, as he crosses his arms up to shield his head as he remains standing.

Trembling with fear, Eric falls to his knees, landing on the sharp pebbles next to the creek, his arms raised in the air.

"Don't even think about it," Jacob warned Brian, as Brian glanced from side to side, agitated and his brow sweating profusely. Jacob could see what Brian was looking at: the trail that was leading away from the creek. He felt tempted to make the run.

"Don't make a run for it, man. I have years of target practice and I never miss my target," Jacob said softly. "I will tell you two shitheads exactly why I care about those two girls. They were my sisters."

"No," Brian whimpered. "That's impossible."

"It's very much possible," Jacob snarled. He rode out the satisfying feeling of letting the men feel fear. It felt good.

"And you sons-of-bitches made it possible. And now it's time to even the score. Though your lives aren't even worth a fraction of what theirs were."

With this said Eric, with a horrified look, turned

to tell Brian, "I knew we should have left town. I just knew it."

"Wouldn't have saved you," Jacob told him, pointing the gun directly between his eyes. "I would have found you eventually."

FOURTEEN

Jacob's memories of the terrible event of fifteen years ago kept drifting through his mind as he held the gun. An odd sensation came over him: it felt like it had just happened yesterday, like someone had ripped a festering Band-Aid off a wound and discovered it had not healed in the least. The two men would know every detail of what he had felt on that particular day, he would make sure of that.

"I was only ten years old when I heard my mom screaming on the phone. The state trooper called to tell my mom that my sisters had been found unresponsive near some tall boulders. An elderly couple out walking their dog had discovered them. The couple called 911 and waited for the paramedics to arrive.

"The ambulance transported my sisters to the nearest emergency room in Anderson's Hospital. Both of my sisters had taken a savage beating and were sexually assaulted. During a heavy rainstorm, four guys offered them a ride home. One of my sisters was able to describe the guys. Doctors tried to stop the internal bleeding. One of the doctors came out to the waiting room to let my mom know that their injuries had resulted in fractured arm and leg bones. Both had head trauma. Their brain was hemorrhaging and there was no way to stop it. Doctors said they were not going to survive the night."

Jacob gave each man a hateful look before continuing. "Before my sisters bled to death, Sarah had given me clear descriptions of you. That was right before Father Samuel walked into the room with my mom to bless them. Mom was and remains brokenhearted. She is still mourning their deaths to this day."

FIFTEEN

Brian continued to stand, trembling and breathing heavily, while Eric remained kneeling, rocking back and forth, crying and looking stunned. *Good*, Jacob thought, *let him feel that way a little bit longer*.

Jacob's lecture wasn't over. "You know what disturbs me the most?" he asked, his voice low and steady. "Trying to imagine the events of that dreadful night. Picturing them struggling and hearing their cries in my head. Waiting for this moment has been torturing me, killing me inside for the past fifteen years. I am sick with disgust, and seeing your nasty assholes still breathing is more than I can take.

"The authorities mentioned something about no witnesses, but I told them, 'Bull-shit!'" Jacob went on to say. "A couple of teenage boys riding their bikes along that same road positively identified you four. The teenage boys were just too scared to tell anyone anything because of their underage drinking and their sneaking out at night when their family retired for the night. Once the boys became of age, guess who interviewed them? You guessed it, your crooked stepbrother, Wayne! He threatened them with incarceration if they mentioned this to anyone. Every one of you shitheads are and remained stupid. All of you just bragged and bragged, like it was just a game, like nothing."

Jacob takes aim at Brian. "Hey man, you don't have to do this. You really don't!" Brian yelled. Eric remained on his knees, rocking back and forth, crying with his head down.

Jacob fired a bullet into Brian's forehead, killing him instantly. "This is for my sister, Brittany." He aimed the gun at Eric, firing a second shot into the top of his head, killing him just as swiftly. "This is for my sister, Sarah," Jacob said.

Both Brian and Eric lay dead. And for a moment, there was total silence. The birds, toads, crickets, and every other living creature had stopped in their tracks.

Jacob had been wise enough to have brought the pair of latex gloves, including hiding the Smith & Wesson behind the restroom building. He was wise to have tossed the pastry box into the fire, removing his prints that would have incriminated him. On his arrival, the only large item had been his Yamaha.

Jacob tried to bury the fear that coursed through him, but panicked thoughts kept entering his head. *This would have just killed my mom if today didn't go according to plan*, he told himself. He frantically tossed the gun into the creek, not realizing that it had landed by the creek's edge. *Better start making my way out of here*, he told himself, as his mind felt like it was running a hundred miles an hour.

Jacob felt fortunate to have bought that gun at a greasy pawn shop with the serial number scratched off. Jacob feared the gunshots were loud enough to cause someone to dial 911. At any moment, Jacob thought, this place would be surrounded with patrol cars.

Jacob climbed over the twelve-foot fence and grunted when he landed hard on his feet on the other side and moaned, *"I have to get out of here fast."* Because he knew that in four hours it would get pitch-dark quickly. Luckily for Jacob, a college friend had once mentioned the park having installed tall fencing, which had encouraged Jacob to hide his Yamaha just outside the east-end gate. He also felt lucky that the group selected this place for their outing. For the past few months, he had been slowly refamiliarizing himself from years past of the park's layout. He'd guessed that if the group suggested a place to camp, it would be this nearest one.

He reached for his bike, leaped on it, and began to make his way home. Jacob was feeling nervous and relieved, but not at all guilty.

SIXTEEN

Twenty miles away from Iowa's state park, and the only convenience and fuel store around, manager Rob says to Mona, the cashier, "It's been hours since this morning's advisory report and still nothing. Wonder if they've caught him yet."

With more than ten hours to his advantage before the prison guards realized Jack was missing, he had managed to have walked a mile from Iowa's state park by 4 p.m. on Saturday. Exhausted, Jack barely noticed the truck that had passed him from behind, had it not been for the vehicle's speed. Jack looked forward and noticed it came to a screeching halt before making a U-turn back toward him. The red pickup truck, bright orange blazing decals streaked down its sides that mimicked fire, was packed with rowdy guys high on pot. The guys had either left or maybe were heading to a party, Jack thought. One of the guys tossed an empty liquor bottle at Jack and another chucked an empty beer can at Jack before the driver sped away. Maybe it was old fashioned of him; he was in his early sixties now, and it bothered him even more that they did not even bother to offer him a lift.

Yes, it was true that he was maybe a bit old-fashioned when he'd discovered his best friend doing the unthinkable..

Another twenty minutes into his walk down the county road, another vehicle was approaching. Jack lifted his thumb up in hopes of better luck this time. The car proceeded to slowly pass him by, then stopped, reversing back toward Jack. A young couple with a baby were the car's only occupants, and Jack wondered what they would make of his filthy clothes and worn-out, torn shoes.

"Are you lost?" the young man asked Jack. Jack replied, "Yes, I am. If you please, I would like a lift to the nearest town to report my stalled car. Died about a mile away from here." The young man turned to look at his baby then to his wife, who gives a little frown. The car window began to go up, and as it did, the young man told Jack that he would summon help, and to just stay put. The car quickly picked up speed and drove off. No doubt, Jack thought, they would be reporting a strange old man walking on the county road. It was time to hide out.

"Let's be real," Jack said aloud to himself. *"My odds of making it are slim. But I'm gonna take a stab at it!"*

SEVENTEEN

Having just arrived at the convenience store, the young couple with the baby ran inside. "Will someone please call the cops? There's a strange old man walking along this county road heading this way," the young man said. "He seemed lost. And kind of creepy. He said that his car was disabled a mile away, but I can tell you right now we did not see a stalled vehicle of any type parked on the road."

Rob, the store manager, as he lounged in his office nearby, rolled his chair to the office door and listened to the young man. He got up and walked out to the counter and leaned against it, then told the young man, "I will take care of it. Thank you, folks, for reporting this to me.

"Now I'm not going to say for sure that this is the convict that escaped yesterday, but the best thing to do is to have this fellow checked out."

The young couple became frightened and anxious to leave. They quickly made their exit to their car and drove away.

Rob was getting mad at the TV station for not reporting the critical news reports. He turned to Mona, the only other person in the store.

"I am still wondering what the heck happened earlier today! I want to know if an officer apprehended the escapee or not? I wonder if this lost fella heading this way may be the escaped convict. I hate this news channel. Right, Mona? Aren't you worried?" Rob stares and waits for her reply. Mona says, "I think you should call the news station, Rob. Maybe they can tell us something."

EIGHTEEN

Darkness was setting in fast. Tired, thirsty, and hungry, Jack began to have dark thoughts of *What the hell now? The law will be making their way for me. My dirty face and clothes made that couple nervous. It gave me away.* Jack wished he had taken the opportunity to steal a pair of clothing from his job at the prison's laundry room. "I just cannot go on anymore. I must hide and rest for a few hours."

Unfortunately, Jack unknowingly selected his resting place within the same proximity where two of the four rapists had been killed earlier.

Jack did manage to get some well-deserved shut-eye. However, within the first thirty minutes of sleep, the events which led Jack into his previous incarceration were the contents of his dream, so his sleep was not especially restful. And the dream felt so terribly vivid, like it had just happened moments ago.

Jack had just returned from a four-week shift working on an offshore oil rig stationed in the Gulf.

Heading home early, flowers in hand and with Helen's favorite pink Asian lilies and a bottle of white wine under his arm; a routine he'd kept for the past ten years of marriage. On this day, Jack's boss had given every employee an unexpected five days off due to an unplanned inspection of the oil rig platform, and Jack hurried home to be with his wife.

Jack arrived home, unlocked the front door, and walked in quietly, hoping to surprise Helen. Instead, Jack heard soft thumping on furniture. The muted noise seemed to be coming from the bedroom. Jack set the flowers and wine on the sofa and cautiously headed to the room. For a moment, he thought a burglar was ransacking the place. Perhaps Helen was not even home. But deep down he knew that wasn't the sound of a burglar. He knew he was familiar with that sound.

When he opened the door to the bedroom, he discovered Bob, his best friend of thirty years, in bed with Helen. He felt instant fury, his blood feeling suddenly hot, yelling senselessly at them both.

In this dream, the flashback of Helen screaming with fright and rushing to cover her naked body. Bob had jumped out of bed naked and rushed to Jack in an effort to calm him down. All he could do was push Bob away, send him flying then scrambling for his clothes.

Helen remained in bed crying. Jack was struggling with Bob, who was trying to run out of the house. He wasn't ready to let Bob off this easily.

He had lost all control. In the heat of anger, he had grabbed his revolver from inside his jacket, firing twice, striking both Bob and Helen. *"Oh god, what the hell have I done?"* he cried. He had sat down on the bed and stared at the mess he had made of his life for a minute, and then he had exited the room. He had sweated profusely, and jolts of terror had squeezed his chest. He didn't know what to do, or what the next step was.

He knew that the neighbors would have called the police to report the sound of gunfire. Jack felt paralyzed. He walked outside and just sat on his front-porch swing and calmly waited.

Jack was awakened from his dream by the deafening sounds of the helicopters overhead. He jumped up and began to run, pushing aside shrubs covered with what felt like blood or a squashed animal of some sort. He looked down at his hands and, even in the dark of night, the source of sticky wetness on his hands was unmistakable. *What happened here? Some poor animal had been slaughtered by a predator?*

He nervously fumbled, tripping over what felt like dead animals. *Please go away, predators, I am not your dinner.* Jack turned his head toward the creek's edge and saw a shining object. He grabbed the gun from the ground but decided against taking it with him, tossing it under nearby bushes.

Panic-stricken, he began to talk to himself in an effort to regain a sense of control. "*What the hell have I done? There's no way I'm going to make it out.*"

Within minutes, patrol cars blocked the county road. There was a lot of noise and activity at the main entrance, and he could hear it from where he was. Jack wanted to give up already, and he was ready to face the fire too. He managed to make his way out through the tight, rough prickly shrubs where a section of torn fencing had been. Six patrol cars with flashing red lights were slowly making their way down the county road toward Jack. The intense panicked feeling made Jack return into the dark forest again, running, falling, and then tripping on downed branches and sharp rocks. With the darkness all around him, Jack had a hard time seeing his way around the pathway. He again tripped over dead carcasses underneath him, and it felt as though he was running in circles. Suddenly, he found himself feeling extremely exhausted.

Sheriff Conner, using the PA system, demanded that Jack give up and turn himself in or suffer the consequences.

"Come out voluntarily or else," he yelled. After five minutes, Deputy Welch exited his patrol car and released his K-9 dog into the forest after Jack. "Go get him, boy," hollered Deputy Welch. "Go get him, Benjy," said his companion and partner of five years. Benjy had a great tracking recorder attached in his collar.

Not able to outrun the strong and powerful dog, Jack was caught in its jaws. Benjy held him securely while Jack screamed. Deputy Welch followed the screams and the growling sounds Benjy made. Deputy Welch apprehended Jack, slapping the cuffs on Jack's wrists behind his back. Sheriff Conner then turned Jack so that they were face to face. "Nice try, now you're heading back to your cell, jackass!"

At this point, Jack knew it was over for him. But the bloodstains on his clothes and body. Who, how, and where the hell is this blood from?

NINETEEN

The following morning, the county and yard environmental truck made its usual way into the park. The men had arrived by 11 a.m. Sunday. They were there for the final cleaning for the season. The entrance gates would then remain locked until the following spring.

Supervisor Raul sent two of his maintenance teams to check the creek area. "You know the drill, get after it," Raul said. His third maintenance crew member, Joe, was taking over the main campground area.

"What the shit?!" Raul yelled. "Either someone is still in the park or somebody just decided to dump this truck here! This isn't a place to leave their damn junk. I'll have this towed away at their expense. Hey Joe, I'm heading to the restroom—I won't be long."

Joe, tired from partying all night and feeling a little lightheaded, nearly trips over two dead bodies. "Holy-moly! Hey boss," Joe yelled to Raul, who was just coming out of the restroom. "I don't think you're going to like what I see here!"

TWENTY

Sheriff Conner was the first to arrive to the scene and approached the campground area. Trailing behind him was the coroner, the forensics team, and the photographer. Upon their arrival, Raul and Joe gave their statements of exactly what they had encountered to Sheriff Conner.

In what had seemed like minutes, word got out fast. Iowa's state park quickly filled with reporters. People in their vehicles stopped along the county road, got out of their vehicles, and gathered around to talk among themselves.

State trooper Martin collected the statements from the second maintenance crew that oversaw the cleaning from the creek-side area.

The two murder scenes were processed, the bodies removed and hauled away to the morgue.

TWENTY-ONE

Early the following Monday morning, Sheriff Conner made his way to the penitentiary to see Jack. Prison warden Tyler accompanied the Sheriff. After the jail-cell door swings open with a loud "*wham*," Sheriff Conner confronts Jack, ready to interrogate him. "You really did it this time, you lowlife scumbag. You're not only being charged with the escape; you will also be charged with the murder of four young men. I need a statement from you as to exactly what happened at Iowa's state park. I want the real story, not this garbage you keep telling the press." As Sheriff Conner turns to make his exit, he glances at the warden and says, "Keep this murderous piece of shit locked up!"

"Sheriff, what I am telling the press is the truth. Those bodies aren't my doing, I had nothing to do with that. You must believe me, Sheriff," Jack pleaded. "I didn't do anything wrong after I escaped, maybe attempt to hitchhike."

Sheriff Conner turns to Jack. "You really expect

me to believe your ass? Are you telling me that all that blood on your clothes came from your own scratches? That blood has been analyzed; it matches the blood from those four young men you murdered!" Sheriff Conner continued, his voice low now. "The way I see it, you're already doing life for the murder of your wife and her lover." As Sheriff Conner makes his exit, he turns and stares at Jack. "This time I will make sure that you get the chair."

Two months on death row had passed, Jack so desperately not wanting his death to be by the electric chair. He considered the ultimate quick way out. One evening, he mentioned to the evening guard that he would be calling it a night early because of not feeling well. He asked the guard if he would kindly turn out the lights, to which the guard complied.

Tears fell from Jack's eyes and his tears became a small puddle on the concrete floor. Jack stood on his metal headboard to balance himself as he tied his jumpsuit leg section to the water pipes that ran along the ceiling. He tied the arm section of his jumpsuit around his neck. Jack pushed the metal headboard away from underneath and allowed himself to fall.

TWENTY-TWO

A news flash raced across the TV screen as Jacob watched the baseball game. "Wow," Jacob said to himself. *It's been six months and the news stations are still talking about the brutal event at the park in Iowa, near Anderson's Hospital.* That old prisoner Jack, he was in the right place at the right time well, for me it was. And lucky for Jack, those prosecutors asked for the electric chair in place of the life sentence. That old man managed to take the effortless way out, and the quick way. Jacob smiled, thinking of his beautiful sisters.

With thoughts of his mom and wondering whether she had seen the latest news report, Jacob decided to call her. "Hey Mom," he said when she picked up on the second ring. "Have you seen the latest news?"

His mom replied, "Yes, Jacob, I did. And you know, Son, those sons-of-bitches got exactly what they deserved. Thank you, Son."

"Yes, Mom," Jacob replied. "I have waited so long to bring justice **for my sisters**."

Printed in the USA
CPSIA information can be obtained
at www.ICGtesting.com
JSHW060759141023
49823JS00007B/74/J

9 781977 235527